Christmas With Auntie

For Pam Muñoz Ryan and Larry Dane Brimner
and Robert (Bob) P James
—Helen Foster James

For Thea x

—Petra Brown

SLEEPING BEAR PRESS™

2395 South Huron Parkway, Suite 200
Ann Arbor, MI 48104
www.sleepingbearpress.com

Printed and bound in the United States.

10 9 8 7 6 5 4 3 2 1

Library of Congress Cataloging-in-Publication Data

Names: James, Helen Foster, 1951- author. | Brown, Petra, illustrator.
Title: Christmas with auntie / written by Helen Foster James ; illustrated by Petra Brown.
Description: Ann Arbor, MI : Sleeping Bear Press, [2022] | Audience: Ages 0-4. |
Summary: Celebrates the special bond between auntie and her little bunny at Christmas time.
Identifiers: LCCN 2022006572 | ISBN 9781534111738 (hardcover)
Subjects: CYAC: Stories in rhyme. | Aunts–Fiction. | Christmas–Fiction. |
Rabbits–Fiction. | LCGFT: Stories in rhyme. | Animal fiction. | Picture books.
Classification: LCC PZ8.3.J1477 Ch 2022 | DDC [E]–dc23
LC record available at https://lccn.loc.gov/2022006572

This book is presented to:

_____

On this day:

_____

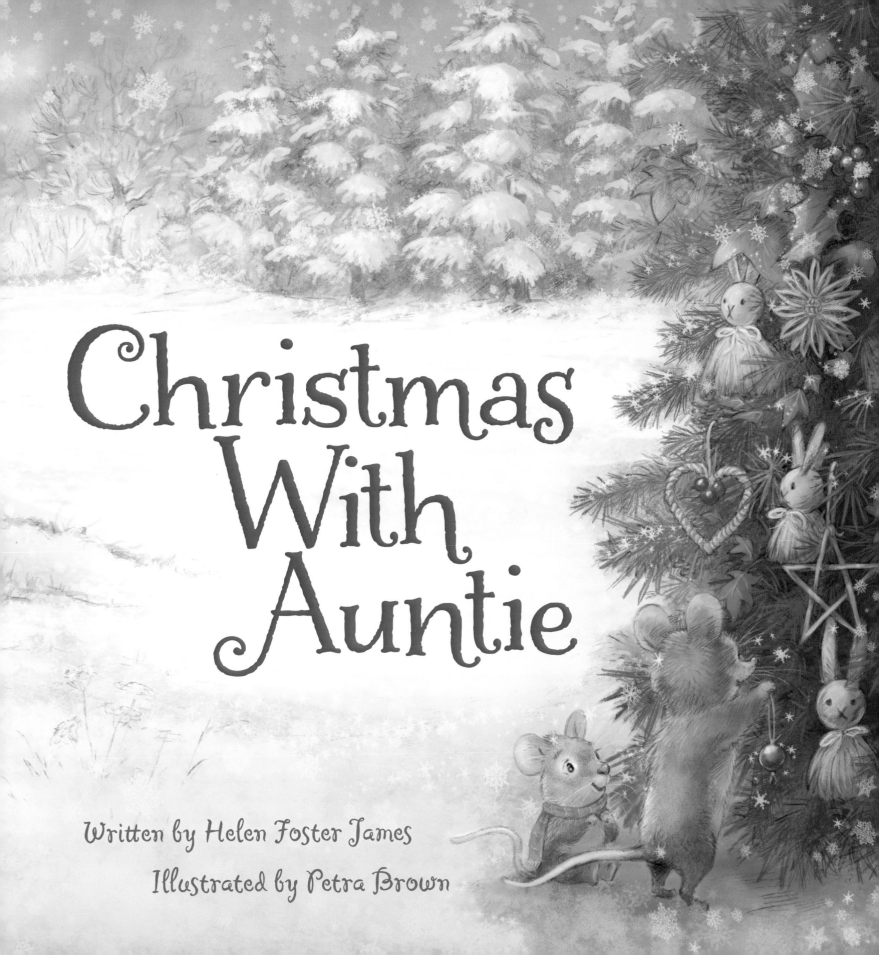

Christmas With Auntie

Written by Helen Foster James

Illustrated by Petra Brown

Auntie is here for some holiday fun,
playing together until our day's done.

Christmas is merry, and we will be too.
Painting and pasting, your auntie and you.

We go together like ribbons and bows,
holly and jolly, and tickles and toes.

Bunny-kins bunny, we'll make and then bake gingerbread goodies, sweet cookies, and cake.

Bundled up bunny, we're ready to play.
We'll trim up our tree for this special day.

Family and friends with holiday wishes.
Mistletoe comes with big hugs and kisses.

Gathered together, carolers singing.
Christmas bells, sleigh bells, silver bells ringing.

Sugarplum sweetie, on this merry night,
we'll wish on a star and its twinkling light.

Candy-cane bunny, my wishes will be
fun times together for you and for me.

I love you, my star,
good night and sleep tight.

May you dream Christmas dreams
all through the night.

Merry Christmas
to My Favorite Bunny

_____

_____

_____

_____

_____

_____

With Love, _____

Paste a picture of
auntie and child here.